Ho-dee-hum.
It was another day at Sleepy Valley Sloth School, and all the sloths were just hanging around.

Once in a while the teacher would remember his job
and wake up with a lesson.
“All right, now,” he would drawl, “everybody yawn.”

Score One for the SLOTHS

Helen Lester *illustrated by* Lynn Munsinger

HOUGHTON MIFFLIN COMPANY BOSTON

Walter Lorraine Books

To teachers everywhere — H.L.

For Branden and Kristen — L.M.

Walter Lorraine (WL) Books

www.houghtonmifflinbooks.com

Library of Congress Cataloging-in-Publication data
Lester, Helen.
Score one for the sloths / Helen Lester ; illustrated by Lynn Munsinger.
p. cm.
Summary: Sparky, a new energetic student at a sloth school, saves her lazy classmates when a wild boar from a government agency tries to shut the school down.
RNF ISBN 0-618-10857-2 PA ISBN 0-618-38006-X
[1. Sloths—Fiction. 2. Schools—Fiction. 3. Wild boar—Fiction.] I. Munsinger, Lynn, ill.
II. Title.

PZ7.L56285 Sc 2001
[E]—dc21
2001024013

Printed in the United States of America
WOZ 10 9 8 7 6 5 4 3

Or "Keep those snores coming."

Or "All together, students, let's roll over."

Most of the time, though, the class just slept.

It was a sloth thing.
They were content in their slothfulness.

Occasionally the principal would drop in and say with a chortle,
“Don’t mean to wake you, but I’ve never in my life seen
such a lazy bunch of louts. Keep up the good w-w-whatever.”
And the sloths would smile in their slumber.

The only movement of the day
came at lunch hour — actually
it was “lunch three hours” —
when the sloths would amble
around the slotheteria
taking a berry at a time,
slowly chewing each one
ever . . . so . . . carefully.

After all that exertion, it was naptime again.
Then the students were off to study hall.

And then it was time for recess.

The dismissal bell rang at three o’clock sharp each day,
but it was dusk before the sloths left school
because no one wanted to get up to open the door.
“Do I *have* to?” moaned one.
“I did it last time,” yawned another.
“My leg hurts,” mumbled a third.

So everyone was happy to go back to sleep until six o'clock when the custodian swept them out, and they rolled home.

One day a new sloth came to school. She had just moved to the area, and her name was Sparky. Sparky was perky. She was full of life and energy and vim and vigor and vitality.
She was a mover and a shaker and a go-getter.
And by mid-morning, she was driving the other sloths crazy.

“Let’s read a story!

Hey, we could use a little music!

Want to build a castle?

Anyone for math?
How about some poetry?"

The lazy sloths shook Sparky off, nudged her with their elbows, and shoved her away with their toes.

So poor Sparky sat in a corner fidgeting on her first day of school, feeling very unwelcome.

“What a bunch of bores,” she sighed to herself.

Then she looked up, and there was
a *real* boar.
At the door.
With a clipboard.

From its outfit it was clear that it was a wild boar.

The boar announced, “I am an official representative of S.O.S. That’s the Society for Organizing Sameness. Wait till you hear what we know about you.
It says here in my report that Sleepy Valley Sloth School is a disgrace to the entire Mammal District.”

The boar was getting wound up now
and began pacing wildly, shaking
trees, whacking some sloths with
the clipboard, and poking others with
a pencil until everyone was awake.

"Want to know your scores?"
Without waiting for an answer, the wild boar boomed on.
"Reading? Dreadful.
Music? The absolute worst.
Block building? Zilcho.
Math? Forget it.
Poetry? Off, below, and
waaay under the chart."

"Thus, I am here from S.O.S. to CLOSE THIS SCHOOL!"
The sloths gasped. Their school.
Their happy, peaceful, slothful school.

They had to do something.
But they weren't doers.
They had never done anything.
Only one sloth could help them now.
The mover. The shaker. The go-getter.
All eyes turned with hope to Sparky.

Sparky addressed the wild boar.
"You mentioned reading. Reading. Of course."
She passed out the books, and the sloths, being unsure of what books were — sandwiches? — began munching.
"READing," whispered Sparky, "not EATing."
She laid a book over each sloth.
The sloths looked like they were reading.

“Music?” Sparky whipped her violin out of her knapsack and played “Flight of the Bumble Bee” while the other sloths snored *ZZZZZZZZZZZZZ*. Very realistic.

"Block building." The sloths were well past their naptime, but they threw themselves into the task. Occasionally a sloth in need of a quick snooze would get sandwiched, but that made the tower all the higher.

By now the sloths were thoroughly exhausted.
Sparky pressed on.
"Math. What's two plus two?"
The answer came in a groan: "For . . . . get it."
Luckily the wild boar heard only the "for" and not
the "get it," so he didn't get it.

"And the last subject you mentioned," said Sparky, "was poetry. Off, below, and waaay under the chart. If you please, we will recite 'The Way of the Sloth.'"
Of course all sloths, everywhere, had been brought up with this poem.
They'd known it since they were babies.
They could recite it in their sleep.
So they did.

The Way of the Sloth

The way of the sloth is gentle and kind.
It hangs from the tree with nothing in mind.
It doesn't make faces, or throw fits, or holler.
It never gets heated under the collar.
It's surely no bother, that's easy to see.
It just hangs around, contented to be.

"That," stated the wild boar, "was impressive. Most impressive. Some nitwit must have confused your school with another. Sleepy Valley Sloth School is a credit to the entire Mammal District."

Off stalked the wild boar.
With the clipboard.
And everyone, especially Sparky, settled in for a peaceful, well-deserved, and very long nap.